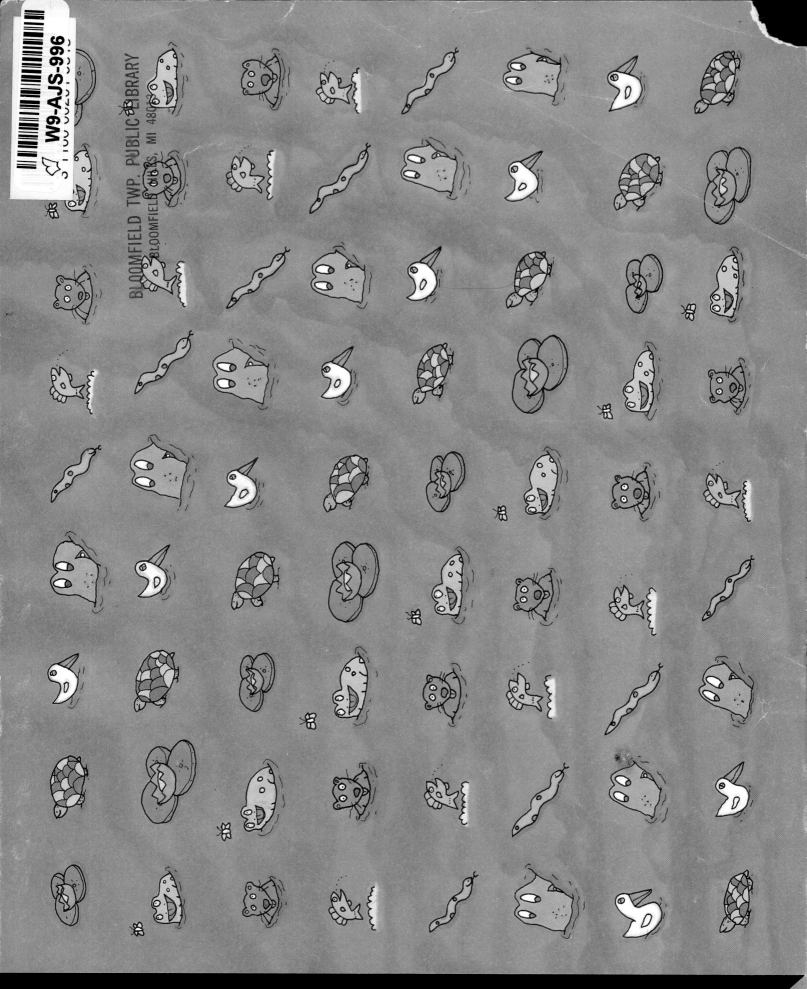

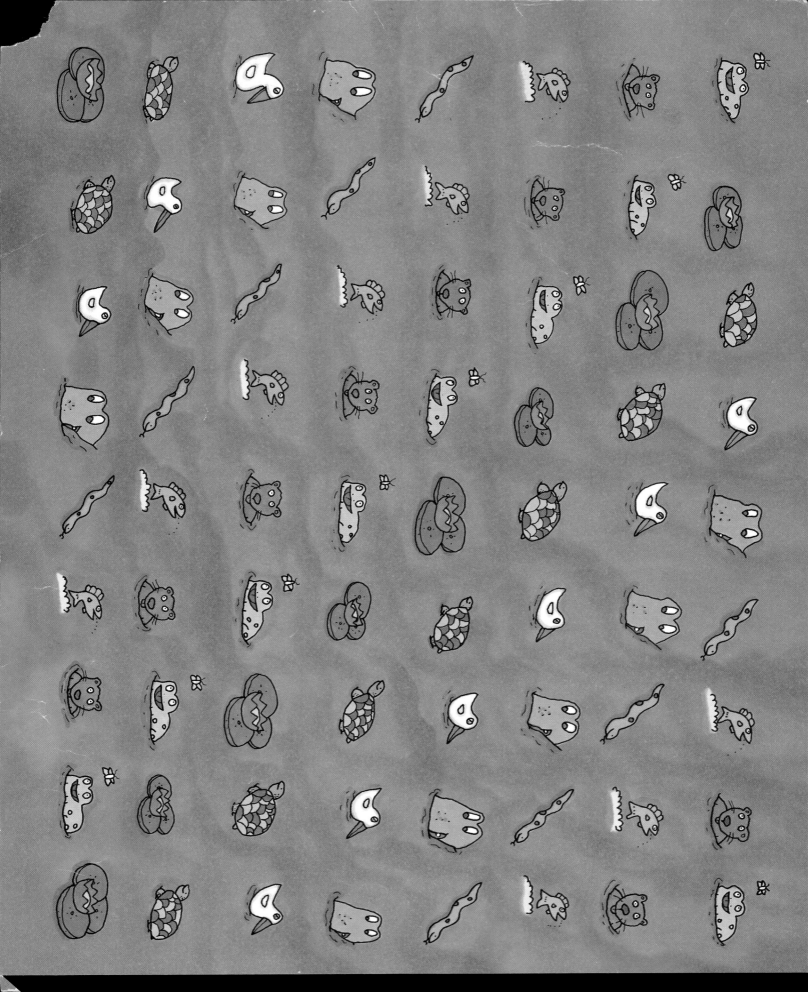

It Came From the Swamp

NICOLE RUBEL

Dial Books for Young Readers · New York

To *the Everglades National Park*

Published by Dial Books for Young Readers

A Division of NAL Penguin Inc.

2 Park Avenue · New York, New York 10016

Published simultaneously in Canada by Fitzhenry & Whiteside Limited, Toronto

Copyright © 1988 by Nicole Rubel

Design by Sara Reynolds

Printed in Hong Kong by South China Printing Co.

First Edition

(a)

1 3 5 7 9 10 8 6 4 2

Library of Congress Cataloging in Publication Data

Rubel, Nicole. It came from the swamp.

Summary: When a blow on the head gives Alfie the alligator amnesia,
he doesn't know who or where he is and embarks on
a series of startling adventures.

[1. Alligators—Fiction.] I. Title.

PZ7.R828It 1988 [E] 87-24653

ISBN 0-8037-0513-1 ISBN 0-8037-0515-8 (lib. bdg.)

The paintings, which consist of black ink and colored markers,
are camera-separated and reproduced in full color.

The alligators were playing baseball. Izzy was up at bat, and Alfie was in the outfield.

"I'm hungry," said Alfie, and he pulled out a snack.

"Yum, yum," he said. But just then Izzy hit the ball hard to the outfield.

Wham! The ball hit Alfe on the head.

"Oh, Alfie," groaned Izzy. "You can't eat and play ball at the same time!"

The alligators ran to help Alfie.

Alfie was knocked clear out of his senses. When he opened his eyes, he didn't know who he was or where he was. "Who are you?" he asked Izzy. All he could see were big teeth snapping at him.

"Help!" he cried, and ran away. Izzy and three of the gang followed him.

Soon Alfe reached the edge of the swamp. Just then a group of joggers came by. I'll join them and those alligators won't find me, Alfe thought.

The joggers took one look at Alfie and ran as fast as they could.

"I can't keep up," Alfie puffed. "I'll hide in here."

So Alfie crawled in a window. As he did, he heard a voice say,

"I'm going for a walk, Marge."

Alfie sniffed the air. Food! he thought.

Alfie strolled into the kitchen.

"Bert?" said Marge. "Did you change your mind? Help me find my eyeglasses so I can finish making breakfast. You know I can't see a *thing* without them."

Meanwhile Alfie sat down and ate everything.

"Bert?" said Marge. "Did you find them? No? Well, I'll just have to do the best I can."

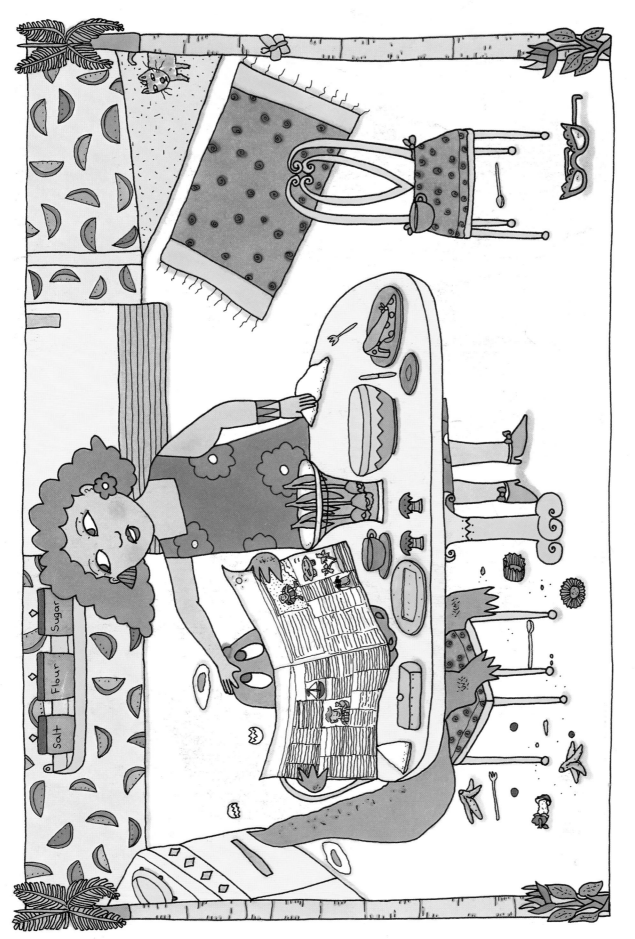

"Are you feeling all right?" Marge asked. "You look a little green. You're cold too!" she exclaimed as she felt Alfie's head. "Get back into bed right away!"

Marge tucked Alfie into bed. She put what she *thought* was an ice bag on Alfie's head. She stuck what she *thought* was a thermometer in his mouth. She was about to give him a teaspoon of mouthwash, which she *thought* was cough medicine.

Just then Bert appeared in the doorway. "Marge," he said, "I found your glasses."

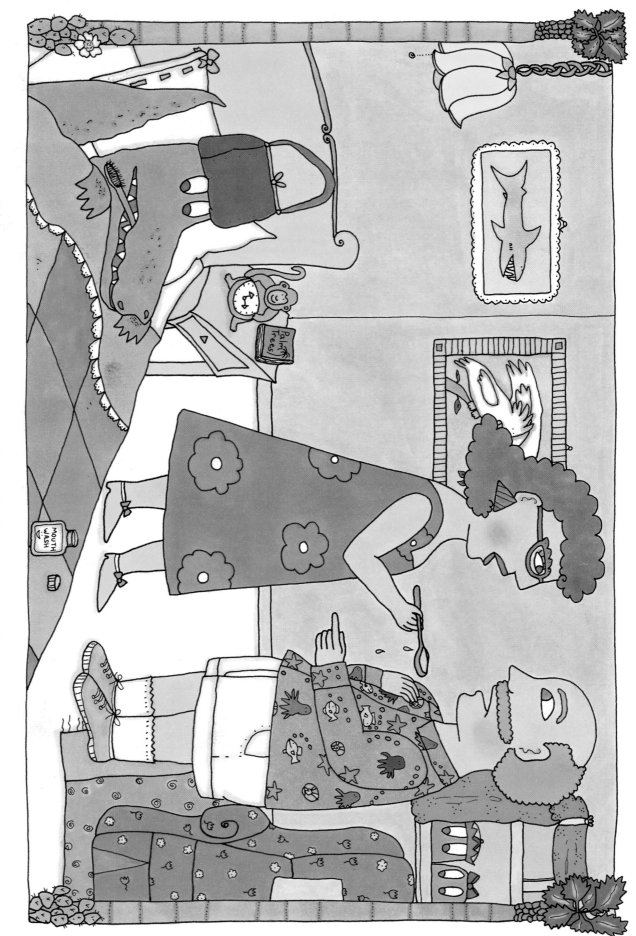

Marge put her glasses on. "Bert!" she cried. "You're in bed!"

"No, I'm not!" said Bert. "Who is in bed?"

They both stared at Alfie.

"Help!" they screamed, and raced out of the house. Meanwhile Izzy and his pals had caught up. They waved at Alfie through the window. "Yipes!" cried Alfie. "They're still after me!" He ran out the back door.

Just then a motorcycle race was about to start. Alfie grabbed an extra helmet and jumped on the back of a motorcycle. As the race began, the driver looked around. He saw Alfie and jumped off fast!

The motorcycles roared by an orange grove.

"Another snack!" Alfie exclaimed. He steered toward the orange trees and tried to stop.

Crash! He was thrown high into the air.

Down he came and landed in the swamp.

"Look!" Izzy called to his pals. "There's Alfie!"

They ran over and pulled him out of the water. The crash had brought Alfie back to his senses. He leaned on Izzy and asked groggily,

"Is it my turn up at bat?"

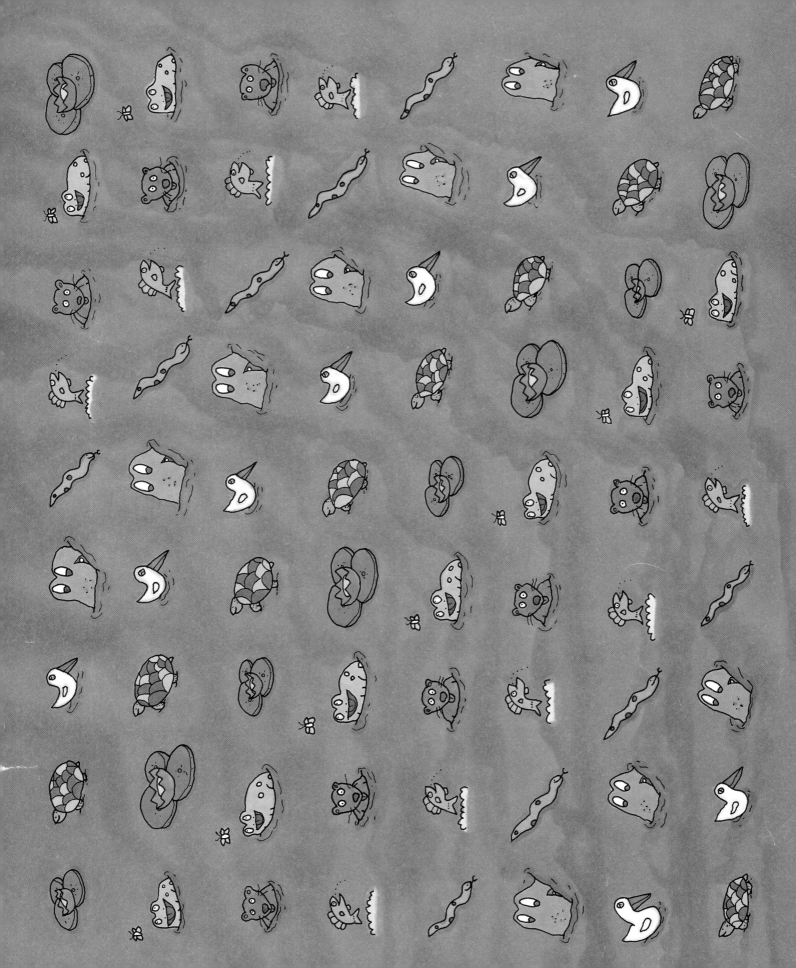

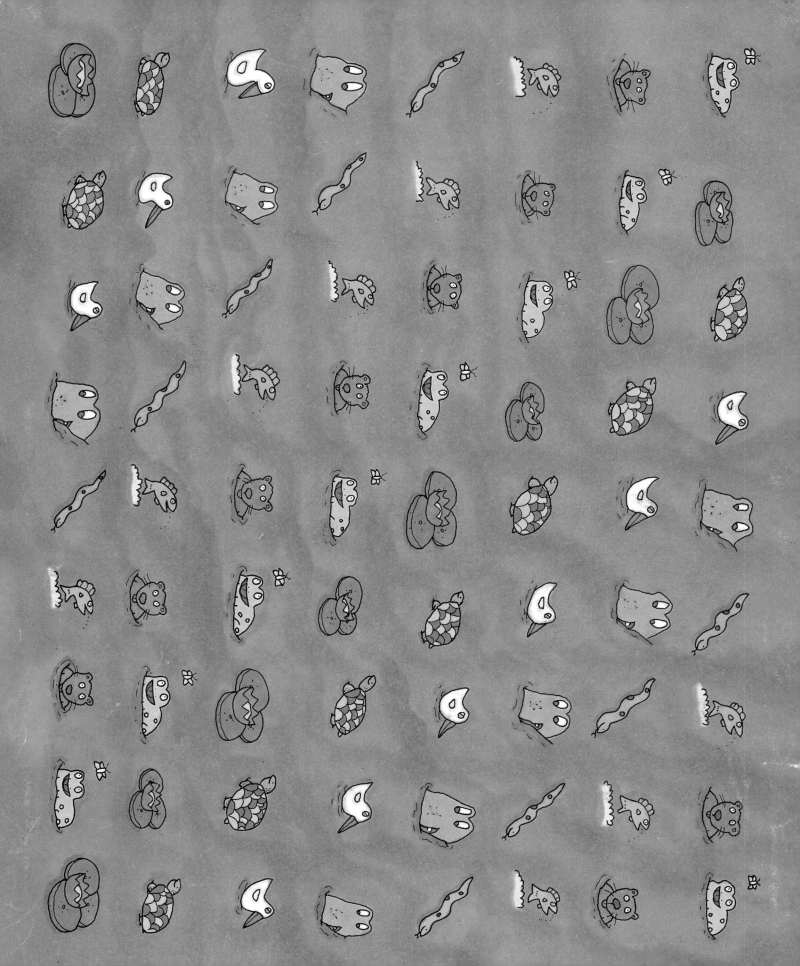